The Hockey Sweater

BIENVENUE
à
STE. JUSTINE, QUÉ.
pop. 1200

Story by Roch Carrier

Illustrations by Sheldon Cohen

Translated from the original French
by Sheila Fischman

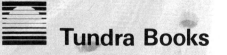
Tundra Books

The winters of my childhood were long, long seasons. We lived in three places – the school, the church and the skating-rink – but our real life was on the skating-rink. Real battles were won on the skating-rink. Real strength appeared on the skating-rink. The real leaders showed themselves on the skating-rink.

School was a sort of punishment. Parents always want to punish their children and school is their most natural way of punishing us. However, school was also a quiet place where we could prepare for the next hockey game, lay out our next strategies.

As for church, we found there the tranquillity of God: there we forgot school and dreamed about the next hockey game. Through our daydreams it might happen that we would recite a prayer: we would ask God to help us play as well as Maurice Richard.

I remember very well the winter of 1946. We all wore the same uniform as Maurice Richard, the red, white and blue uniform of the Montreal Canadiens, the best hockey team in the world. We all combed our hair like Maurice Richard, and to keep it in place we used a kind of glue – a great deal of glue. We laced our skates like Maurice Richard, we taped our sticks like Maurice Richard. We cut his pictures out of all the newspapers. Truly, we knew everything there was to know about him.

On the ice, when the referee blew his whistle the two teams would rush at the puck; we were five Maurice Richards against five other Maurice Richards, throwing themselves on the puck. We were ten players all wearing the uniform of the Montreal Canadiens, all with the same burning enthusiasm. We all wore the famous number 9 on our backs.

How could we forget that!

One day, my Montreal Canadiens sweater was too small for me; and it was ripped in several places. My mother said: "If you wear that old sweater, people are going to think we are poor!"

Then she did what she did whenever we needed new clothes. She started to look through the catalogue that the Eaton company in Montreal sent us in the mail every year. My mother was proud. She never wanted to buy our clothes at the general store. The only clothes that were good enough for us were the latest styles from Eaton's catalogue. My mother did not like the order forms included in the catalogue. They were written in English and she did not understand a single word of it. To order my hockey sweater, she did what she always did. She took out her writing pad and wrote in her fine schoolteacher's hand: "Dear Monsieur Eaton, Would you be so kind as to send me a Canadiens' hockey sweater for my son, Roch, who is ten years old and a little bit tall for his age? Docteur Robitaille thinks he is a little too thin. I am sending you three dollars. Please send me the change if there is any. I hope your packing will be better than it was last time."

Monsieur Eaton answered my mother's letter promptly. Two weeks later we received the sweater.

That day I had one of the greatest
disappointments of my life! Instead of the
red, white and blue Montreal Canadiens
sweater, Monsieur Eaton had sent the blue
and white sweater of the Toronto Maple Leafs.
I had always worn the red, white and blue
sweater of the Montreal Canadiens. All my
friends wore the red, white and blue sweater.
Never had anyone in my village worn the
Toronto sweater. Besides, the Toronto team
was always being beaten by the Canadiens.

With tears in my eyes, I found the strength to
say: "I'll never wear that uniform."

"My boy," said my mother, "first you're going
to try it on! If you make up your mind about
something before you try it, you won't go very
far in this life."

My mother had pulled the blue and white
Toronto Maple Leafs sweater over my head
and put my arms into the sleeves. She pulled
the sweater down and carefully smoothed the
maple leaf right in the middle of my chest.

I was crying: "I can't wear that."

"Why not? This sweater is a perfect fit."

"Maurice Richard would never wear it."

"You're not Maurice Richard! Besides, it's not what you put on your back that matters, it's what you put inside your head."

"You'll never make me put in my head to wear a Toronto Maple Leafs sweater."

My mother sighed in despair and explained to me: "If you don't keep this sweater which fits you perfectly I'll have to write to Monsieur Eaton and explain that you don't want to wear the Toronto sweater. Monsieur Eaton understands French perfectly, but he's English and he's going to be insulted because he likes the Maple Leafs. If he's insulted, do you think he'll be in a hurry to answer us? Spring will come before you play a single game, just because you don't want to wear that nice blue sweater."

So, I had to wear the Toronto Maple Leafs sweater.

When I arrived at the skating rink in my blue sweater, all the Maurice Richards in red, white and blue came, one by one, and looked at me. The referee blew his whistle and I went to take my usual position. The coach came over and told me I would be on the second line. A few minutes later the second line was called; I jumped onto the ice. The Maple Leafs sweater weighed on my shoulders like a mountain. The captain came and told me to wait; he'd need me later, on defense.

By the third period I still had not played.

Then one of the defensemen was hit on the nose with a stick and it started to bleed. I jumped onto the ice. My moment had come!

The referee blew his whistle and gave me a penalty. He said there were already five players on the ice. That was too much! It was too unfair! "This is persecution!" I shouted. "It's just because of my blue sweater!"

I crashed my stick against the ice so hard that it broke.

I bent down to pick up the pieces. When I got up, the young curate, on skates, was standing in front of me.

"My child," he said, "just because you're wearing a new Toronto Maple Leafs sweater, it doesn't mean you're going to make the laws around here. A good boy never loses his temper. Take off your skates and go to the church and ask God to forgive you."

Wearing my Maple Leafs sweater I went to the church, where I prayed to God.

I asked God to send me right away, a hundred million moths that would eat up my Toronto Maple Leafs sweater.

**I wish to dedicate this story to all girls and boys
because all of them are champions.**

Roch Carrier

The illustrator wishes to dedicate his work in this book to his wife, Donna.

© 1979, House of Anansi Press Limited: text
© 1979, Sheila Fischman: translation
© 1984, Sheldon Cohen: illustrations

Published in Canada by Tundra Books,
75 Sherbourne Street, Toronto, Ontario M5A 2P9

Published in the United States by Tundra Books of Northern New York,
P.O. Box 1030, Plattsburgh, New York 12901

Library and Archives Canada Cataloguing in Publication

Carrier, Roch, 1937 –
    [Chandail de hockey. English]
    The hockey sweater

Originally published in: The hockey sweater and other stories. [Toronto]: Anansi, 1979.
Translation of: Le chandail de hockey.

ISBN-10: 0-88776-169-0 (bound) ISBN-10: 0-88776-174-7 (pbk.) ISBN-13: 978-0-88776-174-4 (pbk.)

I. Cohen, Sheldon, 1949-   .   II. Fischman, Sheila.   III. Title.   IV. Title: Chandail de hockey. English.

PS8505.A77C4213   1999   jC843'.54   C99-930341-4   PZ7.C234535Ho   1999

We acknowledge the financial support of the Government of Canada through the Book Publishing Industry Development Program and that of the Government of Ontario through the Ontario Media Development Corporation's Ontario Book Initiative. We further acknowledge the support of the Canada Council for the Arts for our publishing program.

Printed and bound in Canada

19 20 21   10 09 08

STE. JUSTINE
QUÉBEC
AU REVOIR